Robert E. Mack, Maria A. Howyer, Harriet M. Bennett

A Round Robin

Robert E. Mack, Maria A. Howyer, Harriet M. Bennett

A Round Robin

ISBN/EAN: 9783337193225

Printed in Europe, USA, Canada, Australia, Japan

Cover: Foto ©Andreas Hilbeck / pixelio.de

More available books at **www.hansebooks.com**

A ROUND ROBIN

Wings o' Paws
send love
to
Pete and Fingers
and beg for some-
in return

by
M. A. Hoyer,

and
Robert
Ellice
Mack.

Illustrated by
Harriett M. Bennett

Blair. 295.

A Round
Robin.

Introduction

"Oh, dear!" said Princess Amor, "I must really go and see, If the wise old Rook, Is making a book, To send to those children three."

SO she trotted down the Fairy stairs to where Mr. Rook, with a new pair of spectacles on, was busy with pen and ink.

"Oh, please," she said. "You know those children who have come to stay at the Manor House?"

"Yes, yes," said Mr. Rook. "I know! Staying with their Grandpapa while their Father and Mother are away in the warm South for the Winter."

"Yes," said the Princess, "And the birds have written them a Round Robin—"

"Don't I know it!" said Mr. Rook. "It was that conceited Cock Robin began it, and he went to the Fairies to write it; but, dear me, they only knew Old English spelling, and they actually sent the Elves to ask the Bunnies and the Mousies—as if they could tell them. Of course they had to come back to me, and I did it all—and signed their names."

"But now I want to send the children something," said Princess Amor. "All the children who read the Bird's Message, and remember it, and are good and kind and loving. Now, what have you got?"

"Come close," said Mr. Rook, and then he put his beak close to Princess Amor's little ear and whispered something.

"Oh! oh! oh!" cried the Princess, clapping her hands. And then she ran up the Fairy stairs and looked out of the window of her Fairy Palace, and kissed her hand to all the little children, who lay sleeping in the round dark world far below her as it swung round on its wondrous way, and cried softly, "It is coming, dear children—at Christmas."

Wings & Paws
send love
to
Toes and Fingers
and beg for some
in return

Cock Robin

Jenny Wren
(Spinster)

Lord
Cock a doodle doo

Master
Puppy

Baa Lamb

Tommy
Purr

The Hon.
Bull Dog

The Misses
Chick-a-biddy

Mrs Moo

Professor
Owl

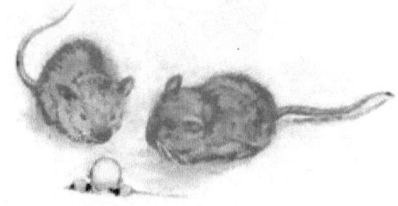

A Round Robin

Illustrated by
Harriett M. Bennett,
Stories by
M. A. Hoyer,

Edited and Arranged by
Robert Ellice Mack.

The Fairy Bird.

"**B**UT p'raps the dickey-birds did do it!" said Baby.

"Hush, Baby," said Patty, in a low voice. "You mustn't talk so loud, or you will wake Grandpa."

"Well," answered Baby, relapsing into a large whisper. "Why shouldn't the dickeys have done it, Alec?"

"'Cause they can't write," said Alec; "and they have no paper, no ink, nor pens, and they don't know how."

"But the fairies might have helped them," said Patty.

"Fairies!" replied Alec, rather scornfully. "Why, you silly girl; there aren't such things."

"Oh!" cried Baby, in horror-struck tones. "Oh, Alec! not little tweety fairies as comes at Christmas and hides in the holly, and hangs pretty things on the Christmas tree!" "Hu-sh!" whispered Patty, "Hu-sh!"

"Gandpa ain't asleep," said Baby, and getting up off the rug, where the children were sitting in front of the fire, while Grandpapa had his afternoon nap in his big arm-chair, she laid her fat little hands on his knees, and peered up into the kind old face. "Ganpa ain't asleep. I can see a bit of his eye through his 'slashes (eyelashes she meant). Ganpa, you's only foxin', and we want to tell you somefin'. Alec says the dickey-birds couldn't do it, but I fink they could."

"What couldn't the dickey-birds do?" inquired Grandpapa.

"Why, write a notice—a Round Robin—and hang it on a tree!" answered Alec.

"And their dear little names all round it!" went on Baby.

"A Round Robin on a tree," said Grandpapa. "Why, is there one?"

"Yes, Grandpa," they all cried. "On the Fairy Oak at the end of the Avenue."

"And it sends their love to us, and wants us to love them," went on Alec, "and Patty thought the fairies might have written it, but there are no fairies, Grandpa, are there?"

"Oh! I won't say that," answered Grandpapa, laughing. "I have never seen them myself, but I have known many people who quite believed in them. Besides, this is Hallow-een. There is no knowing what might happen on Hallow-een!"

"And some birds *are* fairies," persisted Patty. "Why, there is that tiresome little bird who sees everything and tells it to Mammas, and Papas, and Aunties."

"We seed him yes'day," cried Baby. "I'se sure that was he. He's a horwid little bird. Me and Patty and the Gardener's Baby were peeping round the oak, and he came hopping along, and looked as if he had somefin' very 'ticlar to say, only we hadn't done nothing naughty yes'day, 'cept——" and here Baby paused.

"Except what, Baby?" asked Grandpapa.

"It was only a very, very little tweeny lump, Ganpa," said Baby, in a small voice, "and it fell off the sugar-basin—and Auntie didn't see it—and I—I ate it. Did the little bird tell you, Ganpa?"

"No," said Grandpapa. "But, perhaps, he told Auntie Nellie!"

"Oh!" said Baby, in a relieved tone. "I don't fink he did. I 'spect he had just turned round; but, oh, Ganpa! wouldn't you like to go and see the fairies?"

"Yes," cried Patty; "just to creep down behind the trees and see them dancing in rings, and sitting round the toadstools, and drinking out of acorn-cups!"

"I 'spect they did write the Round Robin," went on the Baby, reflectively; "and we do love the birds, Ganpa, and we will try to be kind to them, and the pussies, and everything. Oh, Ganpa," suddenly recollecting something, "we were good to little Kitty. Did you hear how Mother Puss got shut up in the shed all night, and poor tiny Kitty was left all alone and was so cold and hungry, and Auntie Nellie asked us to try and make it drink some milk?"

"And it was so little, it hadn't learnt to drink properly," Patty cried; "and Alec told Baby to dip its nose in the milk, and oh! it did splutter and sneeze and kick, but then it did lick its little mouth, and so it got a little."

"And you should just have seen Mother Puss," laughed Alec. "The gardener went to the shed, and out she rushed and tore up the garden like a mad thing, and bounced through the window and on to the table, where we were trying to feed Kitty, and knocked over the milk. And she caught Kitty up by her neck and tumbled her into her basket and licked her so hard that poor little Kits did squeal."

"But she was awful glad to see her Mother," said Baby, "and we will try to be kind, and—and—Round Robin-y," she continued. "But, Ganpa, I tell you what I fink. I fink that little bird who goes and tells big people things, might come and tell us things about other little children. He must know such a lot of stories. I wish he'd come just in the afternoon, when it's just half-dark, half-light, and tell us pretty stories, when we are waiting for tea-time, and the lamp is not lit. Don't you fink it would be nice, Ganpa—Ganpa?" and here Baby put her arms tight round his neck and whispered: "Couldn't you *ask* him, Ganpa?"

"Well, I'll see about it!" said Grandpapa, laughing. That night Patty waked up thinking she heard a noise in the room, and starting up she saw a small white figure peering out of the window. "Baby!" she exclaimed, tumbling out of bed, and running across to her little sister. "Is that you? Whatever are you doing out here?" "Hush, Patty!" whispered Baby; "don't make such a noise. You will frighten him!" "Frighten who? What do you mean, Baby?" "The little bird," whispered Baby. "I'se had such a *funny* dream, and I'se looking to see it finish." "But dreams are all nonsense," Patty spoke, severely. "Baby, get back into bed: you'll get cold." "Dreams, nonsense!" repeated Baby, in a shocked tone. "Why, they comes true like Nevercomebezzar's did!" "Whose, Baby?"

"Why, the old gentleman Ganpa read about yes'day," said Baby, rather impatiently. "It's such an awful long name, but he grew all claw'y and feathery, and ate wet grass like an ox."

"Oh, I know, Nebuchadnezzar," said Patty. "But was your dream like his?"

"Well, not 'xackly," answered Baby, reflectively, "but it was about a bird, and that's got feathers, you know. The little Fairy Bird, and he came tap, tap, tapping at the window, and he was just going to say somefin', and then I waked up. And then I got out to look if it was there. Can you see him here, Patty?" "No" said Patty after peering through the frosted window panes—"and it's dreadfully cold. Oh Baby—let us get back into bed. I expect it was only *just* a dream." But when Baby saw a parcel by her plate on the breakfast table a morning or so later and got Alec to tell her what was written on it, she felt quite sure that her dream was "a proper dream." For on the parcel was written: "From the Fairy Bird of Twilight Time," and inside were real stories. Baby wanted very much to begin to read her stories then and there, but Aunt Nellie persuaded her not to look at them till the afternoon.

"Then we will ask Patty to read one aloud while we all sit round the fire. You know, Baby, you wished the little Bird to come and tell you them just before tea in the twilight." "Yes," answered Baby, with a sigh. "Yes, Auntie, please take care of them—only I wish it was afternoon now." Auntie Nellie put aside the precious packet till they were all gathered round the fire in the afternoon. Then Patty began, and read aloud the story of The Little Monkey.

The Little Monkey.

"NURSEY," said Miss Lil, one morning. "Father has given me a whole large
penny." "Has he Miss?" said Nurse. "I wonder why he did that?" "He
gived it me for my thoughts," answered Lil. "He said to me this
morning 'A penny for your thoughts, Lil,' and I was just thinking whether I should
put Dolly's blue hat on when I went out, or her fur cap. And I told him, and he
laughed so, and gave me a beautiful
bright penny. It looks like
a gold penny, doesn't it?
And, now, what
shall I buy with
it, Nursey, dear?"

"Well, what do
you want most,
Missy?"

"I might buy
a little totty dolly
for Miranda to play
with," continued
Lil. "Can I get a
dolly for a penny,
Nursey?"

Watching for
the Fairy Bird.

"Oh! yes, I think so," answered Nurse. "You can buy a little china or wooden dolly for a penny, I feel sure. When we were children we used to get little wooden dollies, two a penny. They were not so pretty as the dollies now, but they had jointed legs and arms, and you could make them sit down, and sometimes stand up. I hardly know whether you can buy that kind now."

"Would they really sit down?" cried Lil, a little excited, "because that is what Miranda won't do. She is so stiff in the middle. Then I might buy a chair. I saw some penny chairs in the shop yesterday, and the little dolly could sit in it."

"But if you buy the dolly, you won't have any penny left to buy the chair."

"Oh, dear!" Lil exclaimed, rather in dismay. Her face fell a little, for a beautiful vision of a jointed wooden doll sitting up in a chair was rising in her mind. "But, oh, Nursey, what is that funny noise?" and Lil started up and ran to the window.

"Oh! it is a little dark boy with a hurdy-gurdy," she cried, "and he has a little monkey—such a funny little monkey in a frock, with a cap on his head. And now he plays a tune, the monkey runs about and dances and bows. Oh! Nursey, let us go outside and see him, do, please."

Nurse put on Lil's sun-bonnet, and then they went into the front garden. The little Italian boy came just in at the gate and smiled at her with his soft dark eyes, and turned his hurdy-gurdy and made his monkey go through all his tricks, but Lil was a tiny bit afraid of the little creature, and shrank back close to Nurse.

"Jacko not hurt little lady," said the boy, in his imperfect English. "Jacko good little monkey." "Is he?" said Lil. "Won't he bite?"

"No, no, not bite. See here. Come, Jacko!"

The little creature ran back to his master, sprang on his shoulder, and rubbed his wizened, quaint little face against the boy's olive cheek.

"Is he your monkey, your very own?" asked Lil. "Si, Si, now," said the lad. "The Padrone lets me have him. Jacko does more tricks for me."

"Then I expect you are kind to him," said Nurse; "and that's why he obeys you."

"I love Jacko," the boy answered, simply, "and Jacko loves me."

"Nursey," whispered Lil, "my penny, mayn't I give the monkey my penny?"

"Do, miss, if you like," said Nurse. "I would give him one also, but I sent all

my money away yesterday to Mother, because Father is out of work." So Lil pulled out her bright penny and dropped it into Jacko's cap, and Jacko's master, Luigi, thanked her in soft Italian words and smiles, which latter were much more intelligible to Lil than his speech.

And Miss Lil was really happier in giving her penny to the poor little Italian than if she had bought half-a-dozen jointed dollies, and chairs for them to sit on. She would have been happier still if she could have known how her penny was spent, for Luigi got so many pence that day—people seem in a giving mood he thought—that the Padrone, who employed him, gave him back one for himself.

"That is the pretty little lady's penny," said Luigi. "I know it because it is so bright and shining. Now, my little Jacko, what shall we buy? I know, we will have an orange and some nuts, and it will be the little lady's festa."

So Luigi spent his penny on these dainties, and he and Jacko enjoyed their little treat on a quiet, sheltered doorstep, and then went home to sleep.

Wonderful - Bubble.

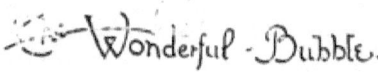

TWO little children sat blowing bubbles one Midsummer Day.

"Look! look!" cried one. "See what a lovely big Bubble; so large, and such beautiful colours. It is like a fairy-world."

The Bubble rose up and up quite out of sight, and then it sank down into the Guarded Grove: and there the birds came and looked at it.

"It is going to open," said the Robin.

True enough it did, and out stepped a Fairy Prince; and, he looking round, cried :—

"Where is the Friggety Frog who knows the Magician's Secret?"

"Here," answered a harsh voice, and the Frog hopped out of the bushes, "but I am not going to tell it to a bit of a boy like you."

"Then I will make you," said the Fairy Prince, and immediately began to fight.

For there was trouble in Elf-land. The Magician had asked a question, and if it could not be answered, ten fairy maidens must be gobbled up by the Magician's Dragon. Yet none could answer it, till someone said the Friggety Frog in the Guarded Grove, knew the Secret. But the Elves had no right of way to the Guarded Grove. Then they caught the Bubble, and sent the Fairy Prince inside.

Long the fight continued, but at last the Frog cried out, "I surrender,"

"Then," said the Prince, "tell me the Secret." So the Frog told

Why there are Two Kings of Pumpundstiefel

There was great joy in the Woodman's cottage. A son had come at last, and *such* a son!

But, as time slipped past, Hans and Margaret grew anxious. Karl was a splendid Baby, but, really, he grew at such a pace, that, even in the parental breast, dismay began to gather. One may have too much even of a good thing.

"He grows *through* his clothes," sobbed the Mother. "Last night I put him on a new pair of socks, and this morning his toes are right through." "You must stop it," said Hans, the Papa. "It really can't be allowed."

"But how can I?" whimpered his Mother.

"I know," cried Hans. "I will make him a little wooden bedstead, and we will pack him in every night: then at least he can only grow in the day."

So off went Hans to the wood-yard, and set to work very busily, and at nightfall he returned, bearing his little wooden bedstead. It was just big enough for the Baby to lie in, with good strong oaken planks all round.

"Now, wife, now!" he cried, "He can't grow through this."

So they packed the Baby into the wooden bedstead, and laid down to sleep with easier hearts. But in the morning Dame Margaret gave a wild scream, which roused her husband out of a delicious nap.

"What ever is the matter?" he cried, sitting up.

Dame Margaret could not speak, she could but point, and then her husband, too, began to shake, and gasp, and quiver. For, behold, in the night, their son's legs had grown *through* the wooden bedstead, and there he lay, with his little feet sticking right through the oaken planks like two handles. Sadly, sadly, Hans sawed through the wooden bedstead, and released him. Then he sat down, and for one whole hour remained silent, slowly shaking his head.

"It is of no use, wife," he said, at last. "We must let him grow as he likes."

So they let him grow, till at twelve years' old his father's clothes were much too small for him, and at last Karl, himself, said:

"Father, I must go away. I am too big for the village."

So he kissed his parents, and set off to seek his fortune.

He walked all day through the forest, and at evening came out near the city where the King lived. The gates were open, and Karl was passing through when the sentinel shouted to him. Karl stopped, and the soldier demanded his name.

"My name is Karl," he answered.

"And where do you come from?"

"From the forest where my Father, Hans, the woodman, dwells."

"And where are you going?"

"To seek my fortune."

"By my beard, it ought to be a big one, to suit your size, my friend. But, first you must go to the Palace. Here come along with me.

"But, why am I to go?" enquired Karl. "What have I done?"

"You have grown," said the man Siegfried, with a grin, "and the King has a son who won't grow; so all big folks have to go up to his Majesty, to tell him how they managed it, so that he may try their method on the poor little Prince."

Karl was rather vexed, but he was obliged to obey. Presently they came to the Palace, and entered the great hall. Then Siegfried stopped, and Karl gazed at the brilliant scene the hall presented.

On a dais, at the upper end, sat the King and Queen, and they were receiving Ambassadors from the Great Khan of Tartary, who were proffering compliments from their Master to King Wisakre, of Pumpundstiefel. And on a stool, between the King and Queen, sat the Prince of Hochsausagerin — a tiny boy — whose name was Otto.

Though the King was listening to the Ambassadors' address, he saw Siegfried and Karl enter the hall, and as soon as the

dark-faced gentlemen had concluded their audience he beckoned the soldier to come forward.

"Who have you there, Siegfried?" he said, eagerly gazing at Karl.

"A big lad, your Majesty, who was passing through the gates, just now."

"Who is he?" inquired the Queen. "His name is Karl, and he is going to seek his fortune." "Have your friends sent you away?" said the King.

"Please, your Majesty," said poor Karl, hanging his head and blushing, "I grow so fast and eat so much, that Father and Mother can't keep me any longer."

"How old are you?" "Please, your Majesty, fifteen come St. Ethelmunda's day."

"Fifteen," cried, the Queen, "on St. Ethelmunda's day. Are you sure?"

"Yes, please, your Majesty," said Karl, bowing humbly to the Queen. "My Mother had no children, so she went to the shrine of St. Ethelmunda and prayed for a son. But when I came she got more than she bargained for, poor dear Mother!"

"And I rather less," said the Queen. "I, too, prayed at St. Ethelmunda's shrine, and fifteen years ago my poor little son came; but, there, you see, he has never grown nearly big enough." "And I," said Karl, "have grown a great deal too big. Oh, what a pity we can't be melted down together and properly divided!"

"Good gracious!" said the King, "what a splendid idea. How tall are you, Karl?"

"Nine feet in my stockings, please your Majesty."

"The Prince is just three. Three and nine are twelve. Half twelve is six. Six feet is *exactly* the height for a man. I am six feet. Would you object, Karl?"

"Not I!" cried Karl. "I am sick of hearing how much too big I am."

"And I," cried the Prince, "of hearing how much too little I am."

"There," cried the King, much excited, "Let it be done at once. A thousand pounds' reward to any man who will manage this matter for me!" There was silence. Then one of the foreign Ambassadors stepped forward, and, bowing profoundly, said:

"Oh, King, live for ever! I will do this deed."

"You think you can manage it?" said the King, all in a twitter. "Who are you? What is your name? Where do you come from? How are you going to do it?"

"My name," said the stranger, who was dressed in a long black robe, and had on his head a tall pointed cap, "is Selim ben Mahed. I come from the land of Light and Wisdom, and I have studied the books of the Ancients—and read the secret of the earth, and the sea, and the air, and the fire."

The Pony
that
didn't need
a Wip.

"And," shouted the King, jumping up and down on his throne, in his eagerness, "You think you can divide these two youths into decent proportions?"

"If you will supply me with proper appliances. After I have consulted the stars and listened to the murmurings of the Ancients, I will do so!"

"Proper appliances," screamed the King. "You shall have everything, everything, only tell me what. Where? How?"

It had been a very busy month. The Physician Selim required many things—a beautiful pagoda to be built, a furnace to be constructed, a large caldron of silver to be cast. All kinds of gums, and essences had to be procured, and the stars had constantly to be consulted, for an auspicious moment. At last the hour drew near. Hans and his wife had been sent for to give their consent, and then Karl and the little Prince were committed into the hands of the Physician, and he withdrew with them into the pagoda and shut the door, which he secured with seven locks.

Then came an anxious time. For seven days and nights, the King and Queen, and Hans and his wife, and the courtiers, and the towns-people, waited in silence and fear.

"I can't hear *anything!*" said the King, applying his ear to one keyhole.

"But I can smell something," said the Queen, applying her nose to another.

"There is something *frizzling*," murmured Dame Margaret, at a third keyhole.

"And, and a *bubbling*," faltered Hans, at a fourth.

"It is like—mutton chops!" whispered one courtier, at the fifth keyhole.

"Or, or mock-turtle soup," said a maid of honour, at the sixth.

"No it's roast goose," screamed the head nurse, who was at the seventh.

"Oh, do be quiet," said the King, impatiently, "how is one to hear anything with such a row going on outside."

But on the seventh day, a sound of strange and solemn music burst upon their ears, and slowly, slowly, the seven-locked door opened, and they rushed in.

There stood the Physician, with a proud smile curving the corners of his mouth, and there, at the end of the chamber, stood two young men, exactly the same size.

"My darling!" screamed the Queen, as she rushed towards them.

"My dearest!" shrieked Mrs. Hans, as she followed.

But as they nearly reached them, both Queen and Peasant suddenly stopped short, while a puzzled expression crept over their faces.

"Which is Otto?" gasped the Queen. "Oh, Karl, which is you?" clammered Margaret. But the young men were

silent. They only smiled. "That is Karl, those are his eyes," cried his Mother.

"But, but, it is Otto's nose," exclaimed the Queen.

"Oh, speak to me, Karl," sobbed Margaret; "tell me, which you are?"

"We don't know," said one of the young men, softly. "We have been trying to find out. I remember the forest hut—but so does—this one. He recollects being fed with a golden spoon out of a silver pap-boat, but so do I. One of us is Otto-Karl, and the other Karl-Otto, but we can't find out which. But we are the right size anyhow, and that's a comfort." But the two Mothers turned in one simultaneous rage on the Physician.

"Oh, you wicked, wicked man," they sobbed, "You have mixed them up so that we cannot tell which is which."

"Well!" said the Physician, rather crossly, "I can't help it now—you asked me to melt them down and divide them, but you did not say a word about their being kept separate. How was I to know? Besides, it could not be done. There was too much Karl and too little Otto—any child might see that."

"But," said the King, trembling, "but what *is* to be done? Which, which is my son and Prince, and heir to this great kingdom?"

It was a dreadful question. All the wise men of the kingdom were assembled to discuss and decide it, but they quarrelled unceasingly, for a whole month, and could come to no agreement.

Then, as a last resource, the King called all the wise women together, and, wonderful to relate, they settled the matter in an hour without any quarrelling at all.

"Of course," they said, "it is as clear as daylight. "It is a case of Twins. They must *both* be king."

So thus it was settled, and thus it comes that there always are two kings of Pumpundsteifel.

THE AFTERNOON CHAT.

*T*HE children were waiting to begin the afternoon story. Auntie Nellie was just finishing a letter that must go by the afternoon post, and Grandpapa was reading his newspaper. Baby had sat herself down on the fur rug with Kitty on her lap, and was singing to herself, in a soft little voice—

> I have a little pony,
> His coat is dapple-grey,
> I never whip my pony—

"Then you are not like Cousin Flossie," said Alec, in a low voice. Alec was netting, an accomplishment his Aunt had succeeded in teaching him, and of which he had become fond. "Don't you recollect how she whipped Samson and made him run away?"

"Oh, yes," said Patty. "Oh, wasn't I dreadfully frightened when I saw him galloping along, and Flossie all of a heap on his back calling out for help."

"Why, what was that?" asked Auntie Nellie, as she began to fold up her letter. "Who was Samson?"

"Samson was the pony at the farm, Auntie, where we stayed last Summer, by the sea, you know," explained Alec, "and Mamma had asked Flossie to stay with us, with Jack and Trots, too, because Auntie Jessie was ill. And Floss wanted to ride the pony, and Mr. Brown, he was the farmer, you know."

"Such a nice farmer," interjected Baby, "he had leather stockings all up his legs, Auntie."

"Those were his gaiters, Baby," corrected Alec. "Well, he said Samson was a very good pony, but that he could never bear being whipped, 'cause he was never used to it. But as soon almost as Flossie got on his back, she began to whack him ever so hard, and he ran away. Oh, my, didn't he tear—and if William, the ploughman, hadn't rushed across the field and caught him, Flossie would have been thrown off, as sure as sure. Mr. Brown would never let her ride him again."

"I don't *like* Cousin Flossie," said Baby, emphatically.

"Oh, Baby!" said Auntie, rather reprovingly.

"Well, Auntie," cried Patty, "Cousin Floss is such a tease. Why, when we were down on the sands—and there were such lovely, lovely sands, Auntie, and then the sea all blue and tossing, with the ships sailing by—she was always teasing. She would come when one was making a beautiful castle and knock it all over, just as we had made it so pretty; or she would creep up behind and throw a piece of wet sea-weed all round your face, or pour some sea-water down your neck; and once she put a live crab down Baby's back, and made her cry dreadfully."

"Oh, it was so horwid!" exclaimed Baby, with a shudder at the remembrance, "it was so cold, so scratchy, and it must have hurt the poor little crab."

Cart Defences

"But the worst was when she nearly tipped Baby into the sea," went on Alec.

"Tipped Baby into the sea!" said Grandpapa, putting down his paper.

"Yes, Grandpa. We were out in the boat with Nurse and Mr Jones, the boatman, and Baby was  leaning over a little, looking in the water, to see if she could see a mermaid or a water-fairy (like those in the book about poor little Tom, the Water Baby, you know), and Flossie gave her a push, and the boat jerked a little at the same time, and over went Baby, and if Nurse hadn't made a great grab and caught her by the frock, she would have gone right into the sea. Her head did, and all her hat and jacket were soaking wet."

"And my mouf was full of water," said Baby, "and I screamed!"

"Father was dreadfully angry when he heard about it," said Patty, "and said Flossie was never to go out in the boat again. Floss was sorry then."

"I hardly wonder that you don't care for Cousin Flossie, Baby," said Grandpapa.

"She was better after that," said Alec. "But I do think she ought to have seen the 'Round Robin,' for when she left off teasing us she used to worry the poor dogs and cats, even the puppy. She would pretend she had something nice and put some soap in his mouth. She made Ponto worry Puss one day, and poor Puss got in the tree, and Ponto barked and jumped and made such a noise, and Patty had to hold him tight while we coaxed Pussie down."

"And another time she got an old tin kettle," said Baby, "and tied it to the other little doggie's tail, and made him feel so bad and ill, that I had to nurse him up all the afternoon. I wrapped him up in my pinafore, Ganpa, and I sung him a song, and then he seemed much better, and ran races with me all about the garden."

"Well, I agree with Alec, that Floss ought to see the 'Round Robin,'" said Auntie: "but now, children, I have quite finished my letter, if you like to begin to read."

The Butterfly's Story.

"THEN you cannot be a Child-soul!" she said.

"Then I will be a Butterfly-soul!" he answered.

The Wise Woman shook her head with a sigh, but she gave him his own way, though as she waved her hand, and he was dressed all at once in lovely wings, all purple and blue and gold, and a body like velvet, and with two eyes as bright as diamonds, she said:

"Even the butterflies have their work to do—even the elves and the bees. They have to be kind to others, and help the weak and the suffering. All, all, must take take the ill with the good, and the bitter with the sweet!"

"I won't have any ill, or any bitter," he cried, as he flew away in the sunshine. "I only want to enjoy myself."

And he did enjoy himself, flitting about in the beautiful sunlight, and tasting here a flower and there a flower to see which had the sweetest honey. Presently he saw two children playing in a garden and he thought he would like to go and play with them. So he fluttered round and round, and at last poised himself with quivering half-opened wings on the child's hand.

"Oh, look!" she said. "Oh, brother, look how beautiful he is! Sure he must be the Butterfly King!"

"It is a Peacock Butterfly!" cried the boy. "Look at the lovely spots on his wings. And see, it is as if he were covered with tiny feathers!" "And the fairies have powdered him with gold and diamond dust," his sister whispered. Just then a voice called out: "Come in, children, dears, to your lessons!"

"Good-bye, beautiful Butterfly," cried the child, as she held up her hand for him to fly away. "We must go and learn our tasks, and you must go and learn yours!"

"I have no tasks to learn," said the Butterfly, as he darted away and flitted about in the sunshine. But presently he grew a little tired of that, and then the sun went in behind a cloud, and he felt chilly and lonely. Just then he saw the Wise Woman standing by him.

"Well," she said, "Are you quite content?"

"No," he said, rather crossly. "Why doesn't the sun always shine?"

"If the sun always shone," she answered, "there would be no rain, and if there were no rain the flowers would die, and you would have no honey. What did I tell you? Good and ill, and bitter——" "Oh, bother!" said the Butterfly, and flew away.

The sun came out again and warmed him, and the flowers opened their lovely cups, and he flew about and tried to be quite happy. Yet something made him doubt it. And there stood the Wise Woman again.

"Why am I not happy?" he cried, impatiently. "What is the matter? The sun shines and the flowers bloom, but I am not content."

But the Wise Woman was silent; she might not speak. He would not listen when she had spoken and now he must find out for himself, which was much harder. But at last he knew why he was not happy, and knowing it he looked around him, and then he saw a little baby in a cradle—a baby so tiny that it had not yet opened its eyes and looked into its mother's face. Then he flew down and settled as light as an angel's kiss upon the baby's lips, and as he did so his lovely wings faded away like a crumbling moonbeam, and the Butterfly vanished quite away. But the baby opened its large blue eyes and gazed up, and stretched out its little arms to be taken to its mother's heart.

"There's the tea-bell!" said Grandpapa, as Patty finished her story. "Come along, children."

They went in to tea, but all the time Baby was munching her bread and butter and drinking her milk she was unusually silent, and her hazel eyes looked full of thought. At last she sat down her mug with a sigh of relief and exclaimed: "I fin'k I know!" "What do you think you know?" inquired Auntie Nellie.

"I fink I know why the Butterfly wasn't happy," she answered. "I fink it was 'cause he didn't want the bother of being good, but somefin' inside him 'bliged him to be good. I feels so, too, sometimes, Gandpa."

"Do you, Baby?" said Grandpapa, with a smile. "Well, I daresay you do, and older folks than you as well. I think you have found out the riddle, Baby!"

The Little
Captive.

All Round the World.

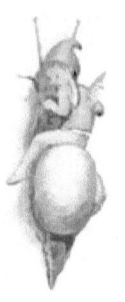

"JICKIE says the world is round," said Miss Moppets, "and if you go out one side of the garden and walk, and walk, and walk, you will walk all round, and come home on the other side. I'll go and see!"

So Miss Moppets put on her sun-bonnet, and took her basket, wherein she put a bun that Mother had given her before she went out, and then she started off by the front gate to walk all round the world and come in at the back. And Snap the dog wanted to go, too, but couldn't get through the fence. It was a very beautiful morning. The sky was washed a most lovely blue by yesterday's rain, and a few little white cloudlets which were floating by only made it look bluer. The birds were singing with all their might, till the woodland rang with their melody, and the fairies had hung dewdrops on every blade of grass and on every flower's tip. Even the slow old snails were running races with a sprite on their backs for a jockey, and the Elves were flitting about on the dragon-flies' backs, and looking after the bees, and being as busy as possible. The fields were full of daisies and buttercups, and up the glade the wild hyacinths were all a sheet of blue. Miss Moppets came to a stile, and there, right over her head, she heard a lark singing clear and shrill.

"Lark, lark!" she cried. "Tell me, is the world round?"

"Yes, yes, said the Lark. "Come up here and you will see."

"I wish I could," sighed Miss Moppets, "but I haven't any wings!"

"Dear, dear! how sad!" said the Lark; and went on singing.

So Miss Moppets went on a little further, and saw a blackbird sitting on her nest.

"Blackbird," she said, "tell me, is the world round?"

"Why, of course," said the Blackbird. "All nice things are round—nests are round, and eggs are round, and you are round if you take yourself the short way!"

"Why so I am," said Miss Moppets, and trudged on again. But now she began to feel rather tired, and her small legs ached, and she sat herself down on a sunny bank.

"Oh dear!" she said, "what a big place the world is. I wish I had brought Snap with me, 'cause he could have run on and seen if it is much further. But I must be nearly round by this time. I think—" But here she forgot to think any more, and fell fast asleep. Now while Miss Moppets was sitting there, she was being watched by bright eyes from behind the tufts of grass; and as soon as she was asleep, the owners of the eyes—the little grey bunnies—came prancing out to look at her a little nearer.

"She's off sound," said Papa Bunny, poking his little nose close to Miss Moppets', and tickling her rosy cheek with the end of his whiskers. Then he gave a frisk, and a hop, and twitched his ears, and curled up his tail a little tighter. "Let us look in her basket. Why, here's a bun, I declare. Come and have a bit, children!" But Mrs. Bunny and her daughters were so busy trying on Miss Moppets' bonnet, that they could not pay any attention to Papa Bunny.

"Isn't it sweet?" said the elder Miss Bunny. "Oh, Mamma darling, you do look lovely!" But the younger Miss Bunny was more critical. "Don't you think," she said, "it is a tweeny bit too large, and hides Mamma's sweet soft ears!"

"It is a little roomy at the back, perhaps," answered Mrs. Bunny. "But—"

Mrs. Bunny never finished her sentence, for just then they heard the footstep of a man who came whistling along the woodland glade; and the bonnet, and the basket were left, and four little grey bodies flashed through the fern, and were gone.

"Hallo!" cried the man, "why here is my little Moppets fast asleep. However did she come here?" And he picked her up, and the basket, and carried her home.

"Father," said Miss Moppets, when she waked up, "I have been all round the world. I went out at the front gate and walked and walked, and now you have carried me in at the back, so you see I *must* have been all the way round. And I had such a funny dream—I dreamt I saw a Bunny putting on my bonnet. But, oh, Father, you've forgotted my bonnet, and left it in the wood!" "Never mind," said Father, "you shall have my cap till I can go and fetch it." So when Miss Moppets

started off again (and this time Snap managed to get out also), she had to wear Father's cap, which didn't shade her eyes so nicely as the pretty bonnet that was left in the wood.

    . . . . .

"What a 'nigorant' little girl!" said Baby, loudly, as Patty finished reading. "How could she walk round the world when there is such a awful big sea in the way?"

"Ah! Baby," said Grandpapa, "she had not had your advantages. I suppose she had not learnt the use of the globes!" "What is a globes, Gampa?" inquired Baby, "Is it a sort of a ship? But—" without waiting for an answer, "That was such a little totty bit of a story. Mayn't Patty read the next?" "Oh! yes," said Grandpapa. "If she is not tired?" "I'm not a bit tired," answered Patty. "Fire away then," said Grandpapa—and Patty fired away.

'Round the world! How shall we go?
  Why, the easiest way!
Just catch a sunbeam by its end
  And hold it tight all day,

And follow, follow over field
  And hill, and dale, and sea:
So round the world
          and home again,
  By morning's dawn
            you'll be

THE DESERTED GARDEN.

THE people who lived at the Gable House had gone away, and the place was shut up. So little Maggie raced up and down the garden paths, and gathered roses, made herself a garland, and ran down to her Father's cottage, where her blind Mother sat knitting. "You have some flowers, Maggie, she said. "I can smell their sweetness." "Yes, Mother," said Maggie, "there are such lots up there; the garden is lovely." "But it won't be lovely long," said her Father, who had just come in, "if no one tends them. Mr. March asked me to see after it, but, what with the hay coming on like this, and Master ill, I haven't a minute of time."

"Father," said Maggie, suddenly, "can't I do a bit?"

"You, lass, oh, I don't know. But you can try."

Maggie did try, for she was very fond of flowers; and, after that, she went weeding, and watering, and tying up; and she kept the garden so tidily that her Father was quite pleased.

"Why, lass, this does you credit," he said, one day. "And you shall have what they give for keeping the place—that's only fair." And off he went. "Oh, I wonder," thought Maggie, "how much it will be. I do so want that book for dear Mother. Martha says it is twelve shillings—the Gospel of St. John—all raised up, so that Mother can read it with her fingers. I have only three shillings in my money-box. And Martha says twelve shillings is very cheap."

But one day when Maggie was busy in the garden, she heard voices. Presently she saw her Father, and Mr. March, the bailiff, and a strange gentleman coming towards her. The latter was speaking. "I am glad the garden has not been left to run wild," he said. "Of course I'll pay whoever has kept it tidy. Was it you, Hill?" turning to Maggie's Father.

"No, sir," said Hill, smiling, "it was my little lass here," and he pointed to Maggie. "And I have promised the pay to her." "This little maid," said the gentleman, smiling. "Well, now, how much do you charge for your work, my dear?"

"What you please, sir," answered Maggie, with a curtsey. But the gentleman saw an anxious, wistful look in her face. "I am sure there is something you want," he said. "Tell me now, what will it cost? Is it a new dolly?"

Maggie flushed red. "Oh, no, sir," she stammered, "but—but—it is a book with raised letters, that Mother could read, because she is blind. I have three shillings, but it will cost twelve; and nine shillings is—oh, such a deal of money!"

The gentleman looked down, smiling at the little flushed, anxious face. Then he pulled a sovereign out of his pocket, and put it into Maggie's hand.

"There," he said, "that will buy the book without the three shillings. No, no, child; no thanks. It is not a bit too much for the work you have done!"

The sixth storey.

The Card Castle.

*I*T was a wet afternoon again. The children had found a pack of cards, and Alec was building a splendid house with them, and Baby sat on the floor and sang in a sweet little piping voice:

We're going to build a castle,
  A castle, oh, so high!
Whose towers and noddin' battlements
  Will almost touch the sky.

But in this wondrous castle,
  Although it is so tall,
You cannot go upstairs, because
  There are no stairs at all.

And in my castle liveth
  A boo'ful little maid,
Who in its topmost turret
  A prisoner long hath stayed.

There came a Knight a-riding,
  His spear of golden straw;
He was the very bravest Knight
  That mortal ever saw.

He cried, "I've come to save thee;
  Come down, oh, maiden fair!"
The maid she sobbed, "How can I come
  Without a single stair?"

Just then came by a Mousie,
  With a mushroom for a hat,
And as he saw their trouble,
  He said, "I'll settle that!"

"Go, fetch the kitchen bellows,
  And give a good big puff,
To bring the castle tumbling down,
  You'll find it quite enough!"

They followed Mousie's counsel,
  And soon that castle grand
Was gone, while Knight and Maiden
  Rode off to Fairyland!

"That is a wondrous ditty," said Grandpapa, "but I think it is time for our story."

MUGS

"*WELL*, you poor little soul, I don't know what is to be done with you now your foolish Mother has got killed in that rabbit-burrow," said Squire Stubbs, gazing down at a queer, big-headed, soft-legged puppy, who gazed back at him with an equally mournful expression. "I just think we had better tie a stone round your neck, and put you in the pond."

"Oh, no, Father!" cried little Peggy, her eyes filling with tears. "Oh, don't! Give him to me, Father, I'll feed him and see after him; indeed I will."

So it was agreed that Peggy was to be a kind of little Mother to Mugs (such was the puppy's name), but she soon found her post to be no sinecure, for a more unfortunate puppy, or one more apt to get into mischief, never breathed. Even as he grew older he developed all sorts of vexatious ways; and at last, after having nearly met his death in the preserves, and once tumbling through the thin ice of a pond and being rescued by Peggy, at the peril of her life and the ruin of her frock, and after every day chasing the young chickens, and dashing into the pond after the ducks, and doing every mortal thing a little dog ought not to do, he was condemned to exile. The Shepherd was to take him to his cottage on the moor, and see if he could mend his manners. Poor little Peggy wept bitter tears, for, with all his faults, she was devoted to Mugs, as Mugs was to her; but the Squire would not give way, and Mugs was led away, looking as miserable an animal as ever was seen.

But next morning there was a grand row in the farmyard, and lo! there was Mugs triumphant, with a broken bit of rope round his neck, chasing the ducks and chickens as cheerfully as ever. He had managed to break loose, and find his way home.

But his joy was short-lived. Again he was captured, and again led off; and for some days there was peace in the poultry-yard.

It was night—a still, dark night. Everyone was asleep at the Grange, when suddenly everyone was awakened by a dreadful clamour below. Shouts, blows, barks,

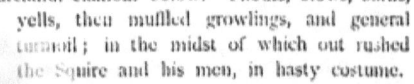

yells, then muffled growlings, and general turmoil; in the midst of which out rushed the Squire and his men, in hasty costume.

"What is this?" shouted the Squire. "Who is there?" But whoever was there did not wait to reply, for two figures were dimly seen jumping over the gate, and fleeing away into the darkness.

"Thieves, as I'm alive!" shouted the old gentleman. "Mark! Harry! follow them! Here, bring a light. What's this?" For he struck his foot against

Very
Venturesom

something soft, which gave a little moan. "It's a
dog! It's Mugs!" he cried, as someone brought a
candle, "and he's half-killed. What is that in his
teeth?—a bit of fustian cloth. Why, the little chap
must have got loose again, and caught the thieves
here!"

"And not too soon," said old Tom. "They
had got the door almost open, Squire; see, here's
their tools, and he got one of 'em by the leg.
Here let me see what can be done. He's badly hurt!"

But though Mugs was *half*-killed, he was not
wholly so; and with great care and nursing he
recovered. It need scarcely be said that he was
never sent away again, and, for the future, was
allowed to bark at the ducks as much as he liked.

The Magic Mirror;

*I*T had hung, that quaint Mirror, in the Banqueting Hall for generation after
generation, reflecting the faces and forms of all who came and went in the
long procession of the years.

But no one knew its mystery or guessed at its wonderful properties, till Clothilde,
that afternoon, noticed a little knob in the lower left-hand corner, and idly put her
finger upon it. Then, as she pressed it, the reflection of her own chubby visage
faded from before her, and in its place was the face of a beautiful lady, gazing at
her out of the Mirror, with deep beautiful eyes.

Astonished, Clothilde took her finger off the knob, and as she did so the lady's
face faded, and her own came back. Then Clothilde pressed it again, and now
there was a grand gentleman, all dressed in velvet and lace, with a sword by
his side, and then a gay page, and then a solemn scholar in ruff and Genevan
gown, and then a priest in alb and cope.

For the Mirror had stored up the likenesses of all those whose images had
once been reflected on its glittering surface, and by pressing the secret spring they
passed in order before the gazer.

Now, Clothilde knelt entranced before the Mirror, seeing one after another of
these pictures and portraits, till there came the face of a Maiden with a distaff
in her hand, and the face looked at her with such loving beautiful eyes that
Clothilde longed to know her story.

So she went away and asked everyone to tell her about the little Maiden with the distaff. But no one knew it, and Clothilde was quite in despair till someone said, "Perhaps old Algith knows. She is very, very old, and has dwelt in the castle for many, many years!"

So Clothilde climbed up the narrow stair to the turret chamber where old Algith now always abode, and asked about the face of the little Maiden whom she had seen in the Mirror.

"Yes, yes," said Algith. "I can tell you about her, and you ought to know her story, for Elsie, the Spinning Maiden, did a brave deed in the old day and saved the Castle. For Elsie was a little Maiden who lived here many centuries ago when the world was a rougher world than it is now. For in those times a great Baron, an enemy of the Count, your ancestor, who owned the Castle then, came with all his vassals and men-at-arms, and besieged the Castle so closely that none could go out, and none come in, so that food began to fail, and all inside the walls grew weak with hunger. And if help did not come soon, the soldiers would have no strength to resist the fierce attacks which almost daily the Baron made upon the walls.

"Then the Count and Countess remembered an ancient prediction that had been made by a great Wizard concerning the fate of their House, and they called their household together in the great Banqueting Hall and the Count said :

"'Will any one of you do a great deed for us ?'

"And they asked what it was.

"'In the turret room of the great keep,' replied the Count, 'There lies a heap of fairy flax, and if anyone, in three days and nights, will spin from it a thread long enough to go round the outer wall, then no enemy or foe can touch us or do us any harm. But the thread must be spun without pause, and having neither break nor knot, for if the thread should snap in the spinning, the virtue goes from it.

"There was a silence for a few moments, and all the women and maidens looked at one another with doubtful eyes, for who could dare to undertake so great a task.

"But, as they paused, Elsie, the fairest of the maidens, and the most beloved, stepped forth and said :

"'I will do it, my lord !'

"But the Countess cried, 'Oh, no, oh, no, not Elsie, for—for whoever shall do this shall scarcely live !'

"But Elsie smiled, and said :

"'I fear not, dear lady. Is not my life thine ?' and so she went to the Turret Chamber and set to work on the Fairy Flax.

"Fast, fast she worked, while the sun rose and shone upon the Castle, and sank to rest, and while the moon rose and wandered amid the tiny fleecy clouds, and while the great stars wheeled on their courses in the heavens, never taking eye or finger from her work, never pausing to eat or drink or sleep, lest the task should not be finished in time, but just at sunrise on the third day the flax was all used up, and the thread was bound around the Castle walls. Then Elsie sank down white and still on the turret floor, for the thread she had spun was her own life, and it was quite spun out.

"Then came a great clamour and stir beyond the Castle walls, for the great Baron and his troops fled away in strange confusion and fear, and the Count and all his household were free.

"But as they gazed from the walls at the tumult, they heard the sound of silver trumpets and the chanting of solemn Psalms, and up to the Castle Gate a procession winded, headed by one who bore aloft a mighty jewelled Cross. And there followed singing boys and men, and the priest in his priestly robes, and last of all four youthful knights clad in white armour, with white flowing mantles, and these had crossed their spears and laid upon them their shields which, too, were white as the driven snow.

"And as the Warder of the Castle asked them of their will, the Priest bade him open wide the Castle gates, 'for' he said, 'we have come to fetch the Maiden who has given away her life.'

"Then with tears and wailing, they brought down Elsie, the Fair Spinning Maiden, white and still with her distaff in her clasped hands, and laid her upon the snow-white shields, and the four knights raised the bier, and bore it after the priest, followed by all the dwellers in the Castle, to the Chapel of St. Agnes, among the lonely hills.

"And there, as the Priest sang Mass, and they laid Elsie to rest in the moss-grown, still churchyard, and the people knelt with bowed heads and weeping eyes, behold, a strange thing happened. For the mantles of the youthful knights changed into great white feathery wings, and as they spread them and rose aloft, and vanished among the flocking clouds, it was said there was a fifth angel with them, and the face of that angel was like unto the face of Elsie, the Spinning Maiden."

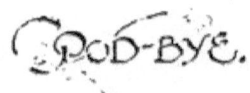

GOOD-BYE.

IT was Spring-time again; bright, beautiful Spring. The daffodils and the hyacinths were blooming in the garden, and the golden and purple crocuses scarcely over. The woods were full of primroses and the delicate windflower; the bluebells were beginning to thrust up their flower-stalks, and the young leaves spread their tender green out to the sunshine. The birds sang all day in the copse, and the cuckoo and the swallows had come home from their Winter trip to the warm south.

One morning, while the children were playing beggar-my-neighbour, the postman brought a thin letter, with a foreign postmark, to the Manor House, which Grandpapa opened as they sat at breakfast.

"Good news, children," he said. "Your Father has got quite strong and well, and he and Mother are coming home as fast as trains and steamers can bring them."

"Hurrah!" cried Alec. "It will be jolly to have them home again."

"And they want you to go back, so as to be there when they arrive. So you must pack up all your treasures and be off. Auntie Nellie had better go with you, and Nurse, to take care of you all. I almost think you will have to start to-morrow, or they will get back first. Why, Baby, what is the matter? Are you not glad, darling?"

"Oh, yes," sobbed Baby, "I am dreadful glad that Father and Mother are coming home. I wants to see them *dreadfully*; but—but—I don't—want—to go away from you, Ganpa,—and—and—" But here Baby so dissolved in tears that she became unintelligible.

"And I don't want to go either," cried Patty. "Oh, dear! Why can't we be altogether always?"

"Grandpapa," said Alec, "I wish you and Auntie would come and live next door, then we could run in and out every day. That would be best."

"Oh, yes," gurgled Baby, who was being comforted on Grandpapa's knee, and began to recover. "Oh, do, Ganpa!"

"What! and leave the poor old Manor House, and the garden, and the Fairy Oak, and the birds, Baby, and go and live in smoky London? No, I don't think I can do that. Besides, then there would be no place for you to come to when you want a run in the fresh air. Don't cry, my darling, you will go home and

be so happy with Father and Mother, and then you will come back and see us for a little time."

"I know who will be glad to see us back, besides Father and Mother," cried Alec, and those are Carlo and Hector."

"Who are Carlo and Hector?" enquired Auntie Nellie.

"Why, our two dogs, Auntie," said Patty. "Don't you remember them when you came to see us, before Father and Mother went away. Such pretty dogs, with long silky hair and big bushy tails. Jane said in her letter they were so low-spirited and miserable when we went away. I expect they will jump up, and want to kiss us all over—though I don't like their kisses much, they are such wet kisses. And there will be Puss, too, and the new kitten and the canary birds—they will all be glad to see us back."

"Ganpa," said Baby, after a long pause, during which she had been sitting leaning her little head against his shoulders. "Ganpa."

"Well, my pet?"

"Ganpa, there's somefin' I want to ask you."

"Go on, Baby."

But Baby still hesitated. "It is somefin' rather big," she said, doubtfully. "I don't know if—if—you will, Ganpa."

"Why, you can but ask me," he replied, "and I can but say 'No' at the worst."

Baby curled her arms round the old gentleman's neck.

"But, I don't want you to say 'No'" she whispered, putting her little mouth close to his ear.

"But I cannot say either 'Yes' or 'No,' till you tell me what it is, Goosey," laughed Grandpapa.

"Well," went on Baby, with a little gasp, "All the stories—that the Fairy Bird sent, you know!"

"Yes—well?"

"Well, Ganpa, I wants you to have them all bounded up into a big book, with pictures in it, and what we said about them, so that other little boys and girls might read them. Oh, Ganpa! don't you think it will be boo'ful?"

"Oh, yes!" cried Patty and Alec. "Oh, do, do! and then Father and Mother will see them, and we can read them all over again. Do you think you can, Granpapa?"

"Really, Baby," said Grandpapa, "that is a grand idea! The very next time I go to London I will see what can be done. But what shall we call our book? It must have a title, you know."

"Why not call it 'A Round Robin?'" suggested Aunt Nellie. "It all began with that."

"Yes, yes, yes!" cried the children, clapping their hands. "Let us call it 'A Round Robin.'"

"The Round Robin that the birds wroted," said Baby, "only" (very solemnly) "I fink that you, Ganpa, and Auntie Nellie were the fairies all the time."

"Of course, they were," said Alec, loftily. "Fairies couldn't do it."

"But it is nice to think there are fairies," said Patty, with a little sigh. "Anyway, we have had a lovely time, and I hope the other little girls and boys who read our book will like it as much as we have done."

.   .   .   .

And the next day was "Good-bye" day.

"Good-bye, Ganpa," sobbed Baby. "Good-bye, *dear* Ganpa, and we'll come again soon; and, oh, Ganpa! don't forget

The Round Robin

www.ingramcontent.com/pod-product-compliance
Lightning Source LLC
Chambersburg PA
CBHW030902260626
47169CB00008B/2639